Jamaica and Brianna

Jamaica and Brianna

Juanita Havill

Illustrated by Anne Sibley O'Brien

Houghton Mifflin Company Boston

For Annie, who keeps getting better
—J. H.

For Meg and Ed, Michael, Jonathan and Shannon
—A. S. O'B.

Text copyright © 1993 by Juanita Havill
Illustrations copyright © 1993 by Anne Sibley O'Brien

Printed in Singapore
TWP   20
4500224933

Library of Congress Cataloging-in-Publication Data

Havill, Juanita.
 Jamaica and Brianna / by Juanita Havill; illustrated by Anne
Sibley O'Brien.
   p. cm.
 Summary: Jamaica hates wearing hand-me-down boots
when her friend Brianna has pink fuzzy ones.
  ISBN 0-395-64489-5   PAP ISBN 0-395-77939-1
  [1. Jealousy—Fiction. 2. Boots—Fiction. 3. Friendship—
Fiction. 4. Afro-Americans—Fiction. 5. Asian-Americans—
Fiction.] I. O'Brien, Anne Sibley, ill. II. Title.
PZ7.H31115Jai 1993   92-36508
[E]—dc20   CIP   AC

"Do I have to wear Ossie's boots?"
Jamaica asked her mother.

"Until I have a chance to buy you new
boots," her mother said.

Jamaica pulled on Ossie's old gray boots. "I don't want to wear these boots. They're boy boots."

Her father shook his head. "They're unisex boots, for boys or girls."

"But they're too tight."

Her mother scrunched the toe of the boot. "They fit fine for now," she said.

Jamaica slopped through the wet snow to the bus stop. She looked at a tiny hole on the toe of Ossie's right boot. Maybe the hole would get bigger. Then she would have to get new boots.

Jamaica's friend Brianna was already there. "Hi," she shouted. Then she said, "Jamaica, you're wearing boy boots!"

Brianna's boots were pink with fuzzy white cuffs. They weren't brand new, but they still looked good.

Jamaica shrugged. She wished that Brianna didn't talk so loud. Everyone would notice.

At school Jamaica jerked the boots off. The hole in the toe ripped wider. She could poke her finger all the way through now.

"You should be more careful," her mother said when Jamaica got home. "I'm afraid it can't be fixed."

"I'm sorry," Jamaica said. She was sorry not to be careful, but she wasn't sorry about the boot. Now she would have to get new boots right away.

"There are so many boots," Jamaica told her mother at the shoe store. "I want them all." She saw a pair of pink boots. They looked shinier than Brianna's boots, and the cuff around the top was fluffier.

"What about the pink boots?" her mother said.

"But Brianna has pink boots. She'll think I copied."

Jamaica pointed to a pair of tan boots. "Look at those, Mother. They look like real leather cowboy boots. See the curly designs? Those are the ones I want."

"Are you sure, Jamaica? Aren't those boy boots?"

"Oh no, they're for boys or girls." They were nothing like Ossie's boots. They were beautiful and they were soft and warm inside. Jamaica wore the cowboy boots home.

The next morning Jamaica ran to the bus stop. She crunched through the snow.

"Where did you get *those* boots?" Brianna asked.

"Uptown with my mother," Jamaica said. "They're cowboy boots."

Brianna came closer and looked at Jamaica's boots. "Cowboy boots aren't in."

Jamaica was surprised. "They're in for me," she said. But her feet felt heavy as she tramped past Brianna. "I saw boots just like yours, Brianna. But I didn't get them because they were ugly."

Brianna looked like she might cry. She turned around and walked off.

It snowed again on Friday night.

"I guess I'll have to wear boots to school on Monday," Jamaica said.

"I thought you liked your new boots," her mother said.

"I do," Jamaica said, "but Brianna doesn't like them."

"But Brianna isn't wearing them. You are. You picked them out for yourself."

On Saturday Jamaica played in the snow all day. Her cowboy boots kept her feet warm and dry. They looked good, too. Jamaica loved her new boots. They were just right for her, no matter what Brianna said.

On Monday Brianna didn't say anything at the bus stop. At
school Jamaica saw her jerk her boots off and toss them on the floor.

"Brianna, be careful with your pretty boots," Mrs. Wirth said.

"They're ugly," Brianna mumbled. "They're my sister's ugly old boots."

Jamaica picked up one of Brianna's boots. "I know how you feel. I didn't like to wear Ossie's boots either." She set the boot against the wall. "But these are pretty boots."

"You said they were ugly," Brianna said. "That's why you didn't buy pink boots."

"That's not why. I didn't buy them because I thought you would say I copied."

"Copied?" Brianna laughed. "Oh no, I would have said they're ugly. I really like your new boots. I should have told you so."

"That's okay. Anyway, you just did," Jamaica said. "Will you get to pick out your own boots, too? When you get new ones?"

"I have to grow out of these first."

"You will. If it keeps snowing for a long time."

"Yeah," Brianna said. "Then my feet will have time to get bigger."

Jamaica laughed. She thought about drifts of deep, fluffy snow. "And we can both wear our new boots. I hope it snows until school's out."